Muck's Muddy Day

adapted by
Lauryn Silverhardt

based on a book by
Diane Redmond

SCHOLASTIC INC.
New York Toronto London Auckland Sydney
Mexico City New Delhi Hong Kong Buenos Aires

Based upon the television series *Bob the Builder*™ created by HIT Entertainment PLC
and Keith Chapman, as seen on Nick Jr.® Photos by Hot Animation.

ISBN 0-439-53921-8

12 11 10 9 8 7 6 5 4 3 2 1   3 4 5 6 7 8/0

Printed in the U.S.A.

First Scholastic printing, October 2003

After a rainy morning, the yard was full of puddles. Bob, Scoop, and Muck had just returned from finishing a job.

"Can we go out and play?" Dizzy asked Bob.

"That's not a very good idea, Dizzy," Bob said. "You'll get dirty, just like Scoop and Muck."

"But it's fun being dirty!" cried Muck.

Wendy was at the farm, repairing the gutters on Farmer Pickles's roof.
"How's it going?" Farmer Pickles shouted up to her.

"It doesn't look good," Wendy replied. "You don't just have a broken gutter, there's a crack in the drainpipe, too. Lofty and I have quite a bit of work to do."

Meanwhile, to stay out of the rain, Spud had been sitting under a waterproof cover in Travis's trailer. When he noticed that the rain had stopped, he threw back the cover and jumped out. "Thanks, Travis," he said. "I hate getting wet."

"I'd better be getting back," said Travis as he revved up his engine to move forward. His wheels spun around, but he didn't move. He was stuck in the mud!

"Oh, I'm stuck in the mud!" cried Travis.

"Hang on," said Spud. "I'll go get Farmer Pickles."

Back at the yard, Bob put on his apron and filled up a bucket with warm, soapy water. It was time to clean the machines, and Scoop was the first to be washed off.

Muck huddled up close to Roley.

"I'm glad I'm not first. I don't want to be washed. I love being mucky."

"That's why you're called Muck!" said Roley, chuckling.

Just then, Bob's cell phone started ringing. When he finished his call, Bob turned to the machines. "That was Farmer Pickles. Travis is stuck in the mud," Bob said.

"I can pull him out!" cried Scoop.

"Your wheels might get stuck too," said Bob. "I think I'll use Muck. Muck's treads are built for this kind of job."

"That's lucky," Muck whispered to Roley. "Now I can stay mucky!"

"Bob, can I please come too?" asked Dizzy.
"All right," said Bob.
"Yippee!" squeaked Dizzy.
"Can we help him?" Bob called out.
"Yes, we can!" the machines
shouted back.

Bob, Muck, and Dizzy took off for the farm.
"Emergency! Woo! Woo!" squeaked Dizzy,
pretending to have a siren like a police car.

When they arrived at the field, they could see that Travis was really stuck.

"Don't worry, Travis," called Bob. "We'll have you out in no time."
Bob tied one end of a rope around Travis's axle and the other end to
Muck's tow bar.

"**Can you tow it, Muck?**" Bob called.

"**Yes** . . . hummpf!" spluttered Muck, struggling. "**I . . . Oof! Can!**"
said Muck, tugging hard.

Suddenly Travis's wheels started to spin, and then they shot forward, sending a shower of mud everywhere!

When Travis was free from the mud, Farmer Pickles thanked Bob and Muck. "How about a nice glass of apple juice after all that hard work?" he asked.

"Good idea," Bob replied. He and Farmer Pickles climbed into Travis's trailer. Then Travis led the way to the farmhouse, followed by Muck and Dizzy.

As they rolled along, Spud popped up, holding a big sloppy mud pie. "Hey, Dizzy, over here!" he called.

Dizzy turned around and Spud threw the mud pie at her. **Splat!** "Oooh, it's squishy!" Dizzy squealed.

"Looks like it's your muddy day!" Spud yelled, throwing an even bigger mud pie at Muck.

"Mud-pie fight!" shouted Muck.

In their excitement, Dizzy and Muck forgot all about keeping up with Travis and Bob.

When Bob arrived at the farmhouse, he found Lofty and Wendy finishing the last section of gutters.

"How are you doing?" Bob called up to Wendy.

"Fine," Wendy replied. "Did you manage to pull Travis out of the mud?"

"Yes. Muck did it, didn't you?" Bob said as he turned around
to talk to Muck. But the digger machine wasn't there.
Where could Muck and Dizzy have gone? Bob wondered.

Muck and Dizzy were still playing in the field.

"If I was as little as you, Dizzy, I'd roll around all day in this squishy mud!" Muck said.

"Wheee!" Dizzy giggled as she flipped onto her back and rolled in the mud like a little puppy.

Suddenly they heard Bob's voice. "Dizzy! Muck! What's going on?" he shouted.

"Um, we were just having a mud-pie fight," muttered Muck.

"We were worried. You better get back to the farm right now," said Bob. "Farmer Pickles has a surprise for you."

Back at the farm, Bob lined up Muck, Dizzy, and Spud, and told them to close their eyes.

"Ooh, I hope it's something really scrumptious!" said Spud hungrily.

"Ready?" Bob asked as Wendy and Farmer Pickles went to grab some buckets of soapy water.

"Ready!" Wendy said with a laugh as she dipped her brush into the
water and started to wash the mud off Dizzy's mixer.

"Ooh, that tickles!" Dizzy said, giggling.

"Arghh!" Muck yelled as Bob lathered the machine with soap.

"Now it's your turn, Spud," said Farmer Pickles.

"Oh, no! You're not going to get me!" cried Spud as he turned to run
away and skidded into a muddy puddle.

"Looks like it's *Spud's* muddy day!" Muck said, and they all laughed.